The Main Character!

The Manga!

#1

Story: Alexander J. McCarty

Art: Kapumax Omega

Color: Aisa Ha

Editor/Designer: Gabriel McCarty

THE MAIN CHARACTER!: THE MANGA! #1 Copyright © 2020 by Alexander J. McCarty

All rights reserved. This book, or parts thereof, may not be reproduced in any form without the express written permission of the publisher. This book is purely fictional.

ISBN 978-1-943733-25-5

Published by Sphere of Compassion, Inc.

https://sphereofcompassion.com

authoralexandermccarty@gmail.com

https://facebook.com/authoralexandermccarty

http://www.instagram.com/gabriel_of_the_exps

http://www.instagram.com/sphere_of_compassion

https://twitter.com/of_the_Exps

https://www.tumblr.com/blog/sphereofcompassion

Artist

https://www.facebook.com/kapumax.omega/

http://www.instagram.com/kapumaxomega/

Colorist

https://www.facebook.com/Arato0696/?ref=bookmarks/

https://twitter.com/aisa_sama/

<u>Introduction</u>

This manga series brings The Main Character novels into a new medium! All the adventures and battles have been streamlined and modified to reach a new standard! To continue the story after the manga, read the *The Main Character!: The Hero's Epic Journey Begins!* and the novels that follow it.

The Main Character! The Manga! is the official manga series for *The Main Character!* series.
I really hope you enjoy!

This book is dedicated to those who feel they are held back by their surroundings and upbringing. May we all break past our limits and claim the glorious life we seek!

THIS MANGA'S PANELS READ FROM RIGHT TO LEFT

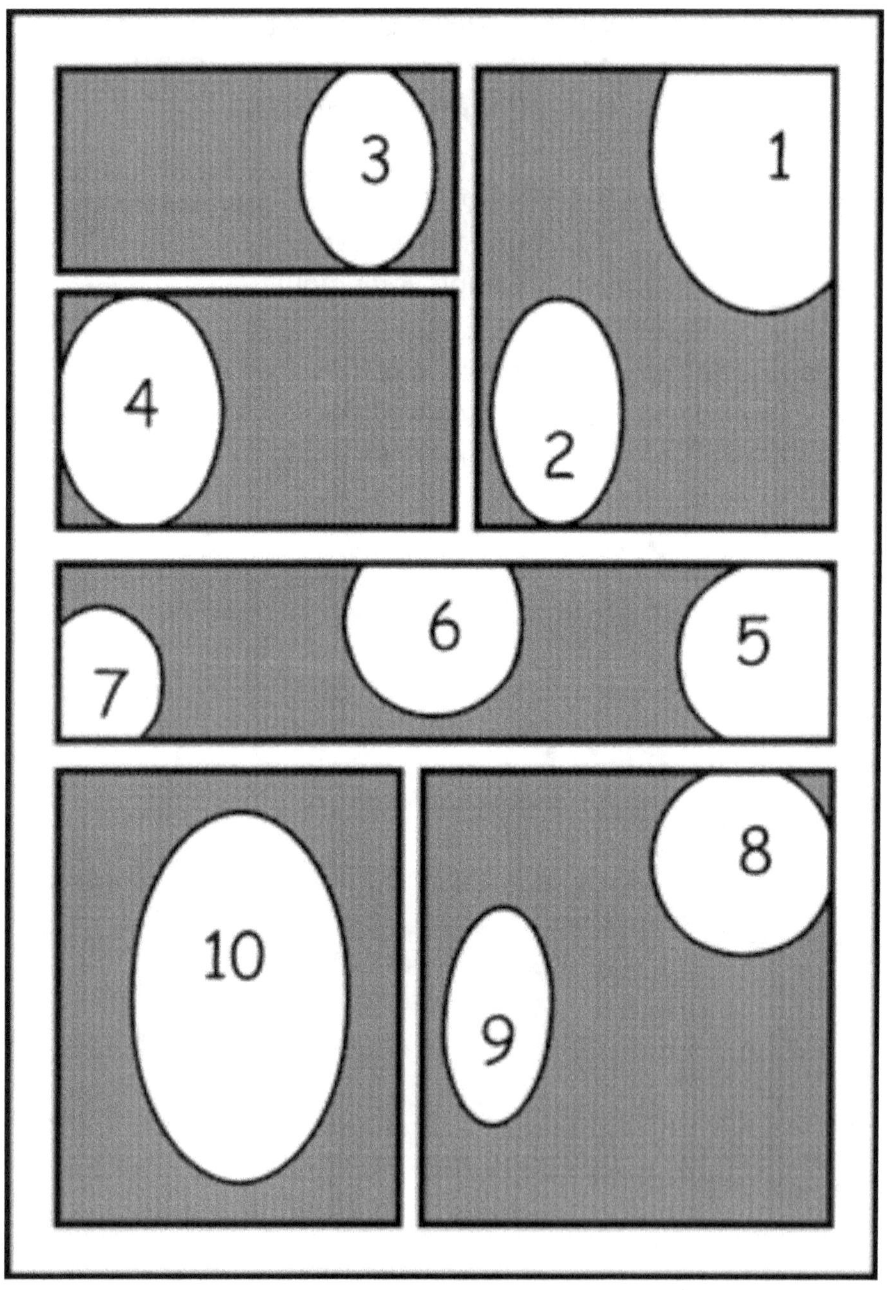

Image from https://mangahejp.weebly.com/manga-how-to-read.htm

THERE I WAS,
WOOOSHH...
OTAKU
HUFF..
HUFF..
WOO
HUFF..
HUFF..
OOSSHH...
STANDING FACE TO FACE WITH MY ARCHENEMY.
EVERYONE WAS COUNTING ON ME,
EVEN IF THEY WEREN'T AWARE OF IT.
WOOOOSSH
BUT LET'S POINTLESSLY GO BACK TO A TIME BEFORE THIS.
NOW THAT I'VE GOT YOUR ATTENTION, LET'S GO TO A TIME WHERE I WAS JUST AN AVERAGE KID ARMED ONLY WITH BRAVERY,
ANIME TRIVIA AND DREAMS OF ADVENTURE!
THIS IS THE STORY OF HOW I BECAME THE WORLD'S GREATEST HERO!!!

DOES THAT MAKE IT EDGY?
MAYBE I SHOULD REPHRASE IT.
I JUST SPOILED THE ENDING. DAMN IT!
NO WAIT,
OH CRAP!
THIS IS THE STORY OF HOW I BECAME...
THE MAIN CHARACTER KING!!!
TRAINEE

♪ I LOOK INTO THE SUNLIGHT... ♪
SSS...
♪ I BURNT MY EYES. ♪
OW! ♪
THE MAIN CHARACTER

♪ I'M RUNNING DOWN AN ENDLESS PATH POINTLESSLY. ♪
♪ AND NOW ♪
?!
♪ NOW THERE'S A SLIDE SHOW OF A BUNCH OF PEOPLE I DON'T KNOW. ♪
OTAKU
FIST CLENCH
♪ AND IT'S RUINING WHO JOINS MY TEAM. DAMN SPOILERS! ♪

♪ THAT'S SO DEEP! ♪
OTAKU
♪ THEN MY HAND IS REACHING OUT TO THE SKY. ♪
♪ NOW ALL THE VILLAINS ARE TAKING UP MY SCREEN TIME! ♪
♪ I JUMP IN AND PUNCH THEM WITH MY SPIKY HAIR. ♪
♪ BUT THEN ♪

I'M NOW CLENCHING MY FIST ON TOP OF A MOUNTAIN OF GRAVES. HOLY SHIT, THAT'S SOME AWESOME SYMBOLISM!
OTAKU
RIP
I'M THEN KNOCKED BACK.
I WIPE THE BLOOD OFF MY CHEEK.

AND THEN I RUN FORTH AND PUNCH WITH ALL MY MIGHT!
NO MATTER WHAT I WONT DIE! AND THERE'S ONLY ONE REASON WHY.
TAKU
IT'S BECAUSE I'M THE MAIN CHARACTER! ME ME ME! I'M THE MAIN CHARACTER!
HELL YEAH! I'M THE MAIN CHARACTER!!!...

CHAPTER 1 - THE LEGEND RE-BEGINS ONCE AGAIN

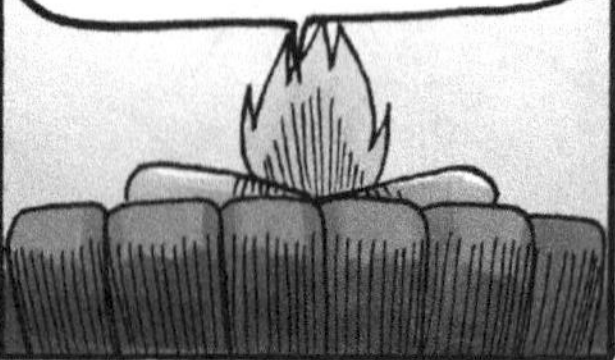

AWW, HE'S LIKE A CLAWLESS KITTEN WHEN HE'S LIKE THIS.
OTAKU

PUT THAT FROWN AWAY!!!
BUWAHAHA!!
TICKLE TICKLE TICKLE
S-S-STOPP!!!

SORRY FOR BEING SO... NEGATIVE
HOW CAN I HELP?
DO YOU THINK THAT SONG WILL WORK FOR OUR VIRALTUBE OPENING IF I SPLICE IN SOME CLIPS FROM PREVIOUS EPISODES?

SMILE

OTAKU
HIS EYES ARE SO PRETTY ...

YOUR DEVOTION SHALL GIVE IT NEW LIFE.

DAMN, I KIND OF JUST THREW MY AUDIENCE IN THE MIDDLE OF A SCENE WITHOUT ANY EXPOSITION. MY NAME IS MAIN CHARACTER. BOTH MY PARENTS ARE GONE, SO NOBODY KNOWS MY REAL NAME. I CHOSE THIS NAME, AND HOPEFULLY IT WILL GIVE ME THE POWER TO CHOOSE MY OWN DESTINY.

MAIN CHARACTER

VIRALTUBE LEGEND; OTAKU SAGE

I LOOK ABOUT AS ASIAN AS MOST ANIME HEROES. OH YEAH, I'M ALSO A SADOMASOCHIST AND A DELIQUENT. I BELIEVE IN JUSTICE TOO, LIKE ALL GOOD HEROES.

OH, AND I'M REALLY LAID BACK AND COOL. I GOT THESE SEXY MUSCLES FROM SPARRING WITH MY BESTFRIEND JUST LIKE A CERTAIN BROTHERLY DUO OF ALCHEMISTS.

HANDS: SCARS FROM INTENSE BATTLES OVER COPYRIGHT DISPUTES

NAVAL: STARS-SHAPED BIRTHMARK

CROTCH: SOURCE OF OTAKU POWER

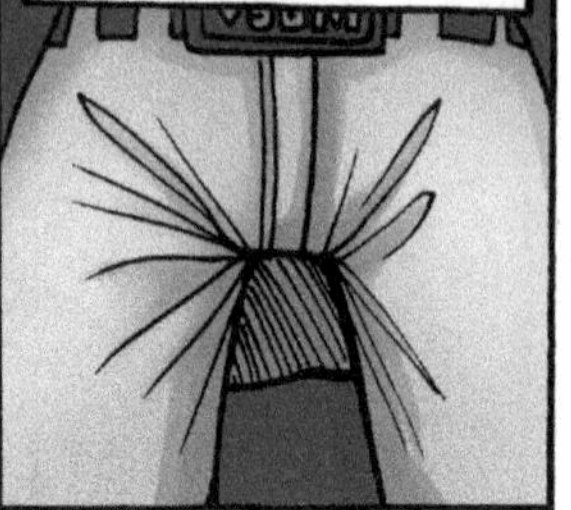

CHEST: MOST LIKELY RIDDLED WITH HOLES IN THE SHAPE OF A CONSTELLATION

ARMS: MUSCULAR PROM SPARRING WITH BF

STOMACH: BLACKHOLE

BRAIN: A DATA BASE OF ANIME FACTS AND THEORIES

FACE: CLEARLY ASIAN

HAIR: PROOF OF PROTAGONIST RANK

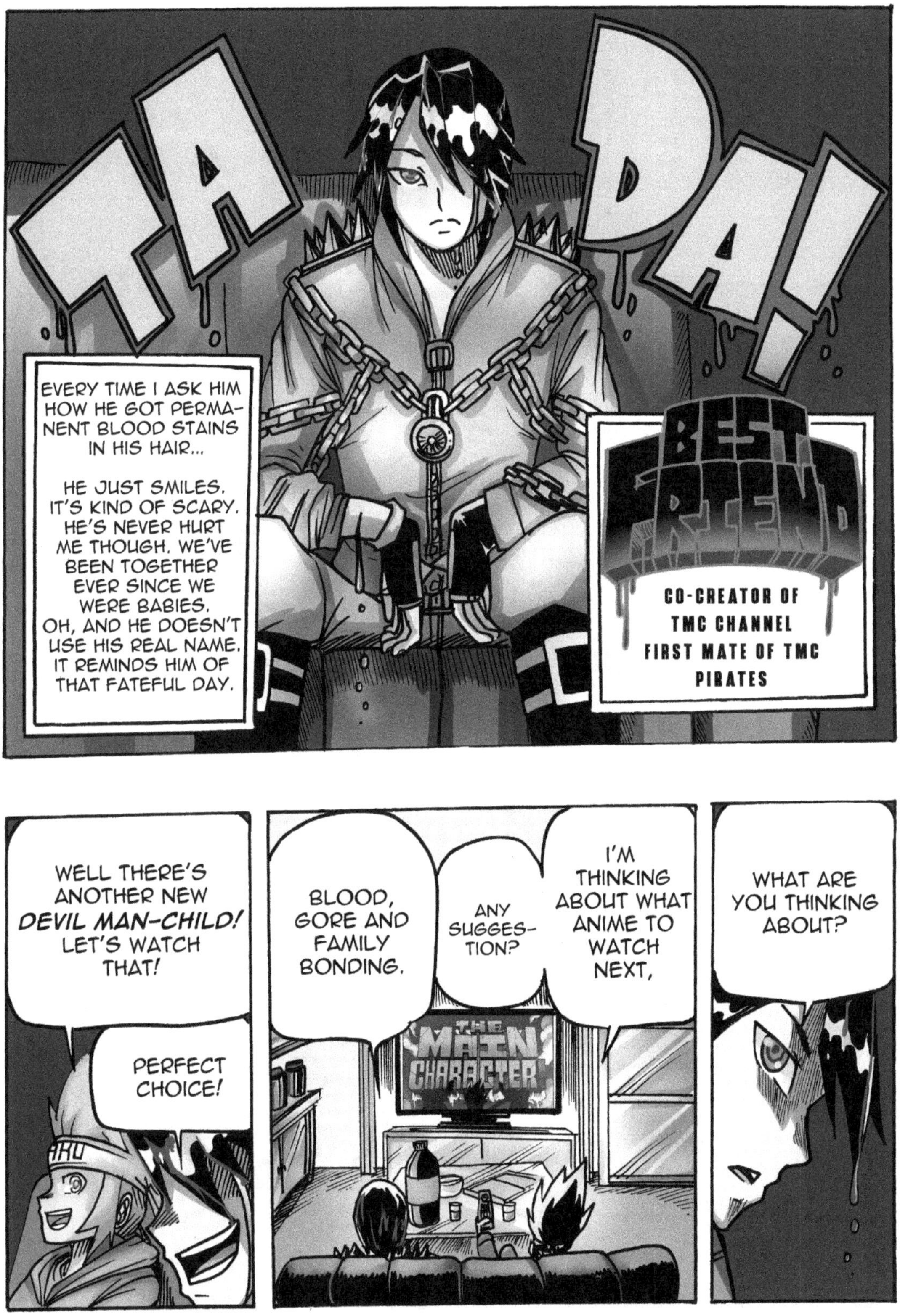

TA DA!

EVERY TIME I ASK HIM HOW HE GOT PERMANENT BLOOD STAINS IN HIS HAIR...

HE JUST SMILES. IT'S KIND OF SCARY. HE'S NEVER HURT ME THOUGH. WE'VE BEEN TOGETHER EVER SINCE WE WERE BABIES. OH, AND HE DOESN'T USE HIS REAL NAME. IT REMINDS HIM OF THAT FATEFUL DAY.

BEST FRIEND

CO-CREATOR OF TMC CHANNEL

FIRST MATE OF TMC PIRATES

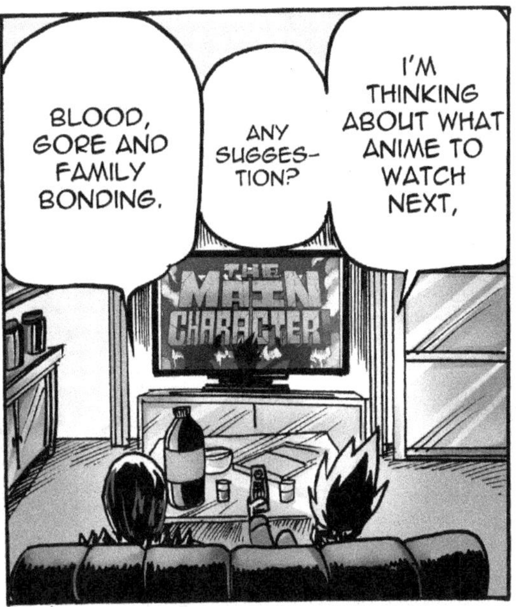

IT'S JEREMY'S BIRTHDAY TODAY!
MAIN...

WHY ARE YOU HERE !?
OLD HAG
OWNER OF LOST KEYS ORPHANAGE; SECRET OCCUPATION PRISON WARDEN
THE WOMAN'S NAME WAS LINDA, BUT I HAVE MY OWN NICKNAME FOR HER. SINCE SHE'S SLIGHTLY RELEVANT, I'LL GIVE HER A CHARACTER INTRO.

YOU KNOW HOW MUCH I HATE BIRTHDAYS.

DRILL DRILL
IT WOULD BE GOOD FOR YOU TO SPEND TIME WITH THE OTHER KIDS. IT'S JEREMY'S BIRTHDAY.

SADLY, I'VE ALWAYS HAD FOUR TIMES LESS PRESENTS THAN THE OTHER KIDS.
BEING UNIQUE AND AWESOME HAS SOME MAJOR DOWNSIDES TO IT.
THE TRUTH IS I AM ACTUALLY ONLY FOUR YEARS OLD!
I KNOW, I'M HOT!
THE REASON I DON'T LOOK FOUR IS BECAUSE I WAS BORN ON A LEAP YEAR.

WE ARE GOING TO HAVE SOME VEGAN CUPCAKES AFTER BREAKFAST.
IT WOULD MEAN A LOT TO HIM
IF YOU SHOWED UP.

AFTER THE OPENING SONG.
OKAY?
OTAKU
HOLY ***SANGOKU***, THEY HAVE CUPCAKES!

I CAN'T BEAR TO LOOK INTO THOSE DISAPPRO-VING EYES.
YOU'VE BEEN CHEATING,
HAVEN'T YOU?
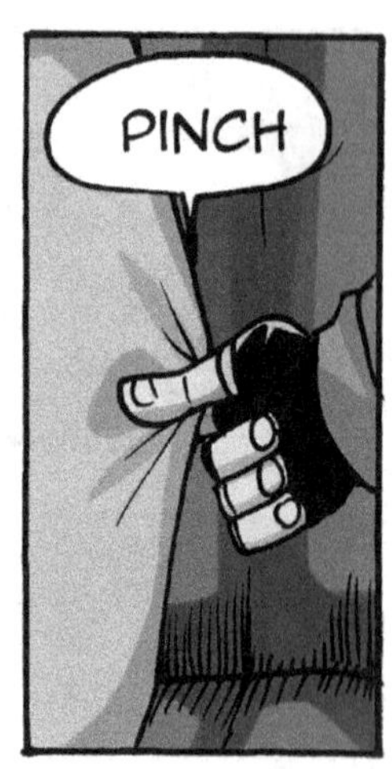
PINCH

EESH! UNLIKE HER, HE KNOWS HOT TO GUILT TRIP ME.
OTAKU

YOU THOUGHT I WOULDN'T NOTICE.

I WANT YOU TO RESPECT ME AND THE OTHER ORPHANS.
WHAT DO YOU WANT WOMAN?
CLICK

YOUR HEALTH IS A SERIOUS THING.
OTAKU

I CAN'T HELP BUT LIKE SWEETS.
I'M A TEENAGER.
TSUNDERES AND MUSCLE MEN LOVE SWEETS. YOU'RE NEITHER, SO DON'T PRETEND IT'S PART OF YOUR LARPING ALIAS.

OH CRAP! DID I MENTION THAT I LIVE AT AN ORPHANAGE? **LOST KEYS ORPHANAGE** IS A RUNDOWN UGLY GREY BUILDING WHERE KIDS GET DROPPED OFF AS OFTEN AS THEY LEAVE. I COULDN'T CARE LESS WHICH GENERIC KID IS JEREMY. SIDE CHARACTERS COME AND GO ANYWAYS, SO WHY BOTHER MAKING FRIENDS?

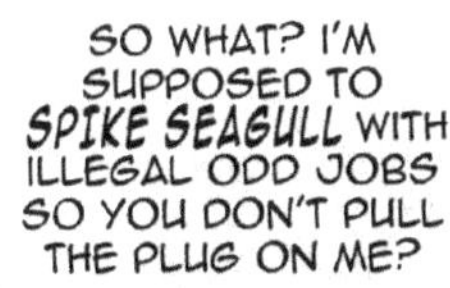

MY CHAKRA FLOW STOPPED LIKE THE PHANORAMIC ACTION SHOTS FROM **VERY TAIL**

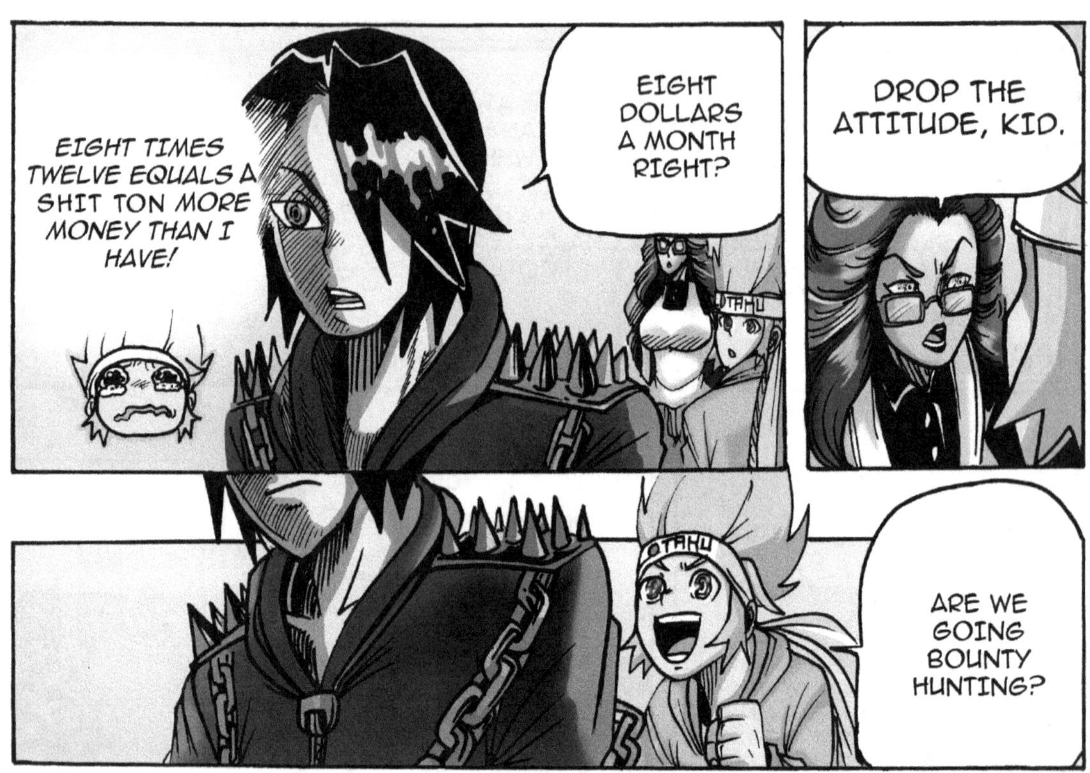
EIGHT TIMES TWELVE EQUALS A SHIT TON MORE MONEY THAN I HAVE!
EIGHT DOLLARS A MONTH RIGHT?
OTAKU
DROP THE ATTITUDE, KID.
OTAKU
ARE WE GOING BOUNTY HUNTING?

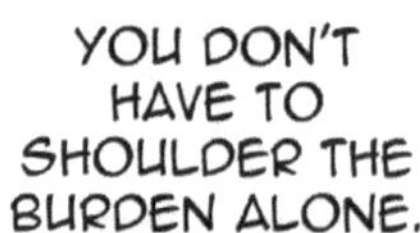
YOU DON'T HAVE TO SHOULDER THE BURDEN ALONE.
WE'RE A TWO-MAN *SUPAH SENTAI.*

I WILL RETURN.
OTAKU

MARTIAL ARTS ARE FOR SELF-DEFENSE NOT GAUDY TOURNAMENTS OR VIGILANTE WORK.
YOU'VE BEEN TRAINING ME! I'M READY TO GO OUT CRIME FIGHTING WITH YOU.
SLICE
PUNCH!

YOU'RE STAYING HOME TO SET UP OUR QUEUE FOR THE MONTH.

I'M GOING TO GET YOU THE MONEY.
THAT GAZE MAKES ME TREMBLE.

ANIME IS OUR ONLY ESCAPE FROM A WORLD THAT SEES US AS DISCARDED TRASH. TAKING THAT AWAY IS LIKE TAKING A CHILD AWAY FROM THEIR PARENTS.

HOLD UP!

WE GOTTA GO IF WE DON'T WANT TO MISS THE BUS.

WHAT ABOUT BREAK-FAST?
NO NEED. I'LL FEED HIM WHEN I RETURN.
I WISH HE WOULDN'T BABY ME ALL THE TIME.
NOM NOM

THIS IS MY STORY AND I DON'T WANT YOU MISSING HALF OF IT BECAUSE OF A SHOPPING IMPULSE.
NO PRODUCT PLACEMENT ALOWWED.
LET THE PROGRAM RESUME.
AND NOW FOR A QUICK COMMERCIAL BREAK.
JUST KIDDING!

YOU'RE PROBABLY WONDERING WHAT KIND OF BADASS SCHOOL THE MAIN CHARACTER GOES TO. SADLY, IT'S NOTHING SPECIAL. THERE ARE NO TEACHERS WHO TEACH ELITIST KIDS HOW TO USE THEIR SUPER POWERS;

NO NINJA EXAMS AND IT'S NOT AN ALL-GIRLS SCHOOL WHERE I'M THE ONLY BOY EITHER. IT'S A BORING NORMAL GRADE SCHOOL CALLED ***WATSON ELEMENTARY***. I'M CURRENTLY REPEATING THE THIRD GRADE FOR THE SIXTH TIME.

I'VE LOST TRACK OF HOW MANY YEARS I'VE BEEN STUCK IN THIS STALE CLASSROOM. THE ONLY THING UNIQUE ABOUT THE CLASSROOM IS THE SEVEN YEAR OLD COLLEGE STUDENT WE HAVE FOR A TEACHER. HE'S CURRENTLY TEACHING US HOW TO GET A GRANT FOR HAVING MULTIPLE INTERNSHIPS OR SOMETHING. LITTLE MORON DOESN'T REALIZE HE'S SPEAKING TO A BUNCH OF GRADE-SCHOOLERS.

MY MOTHER GAVE BIRTH ON A TRAIN.

I AM SPECIAL! JUST LIKE THE OG BLACK SWORDSMAN, I WAS BORN AN ORPHAN.
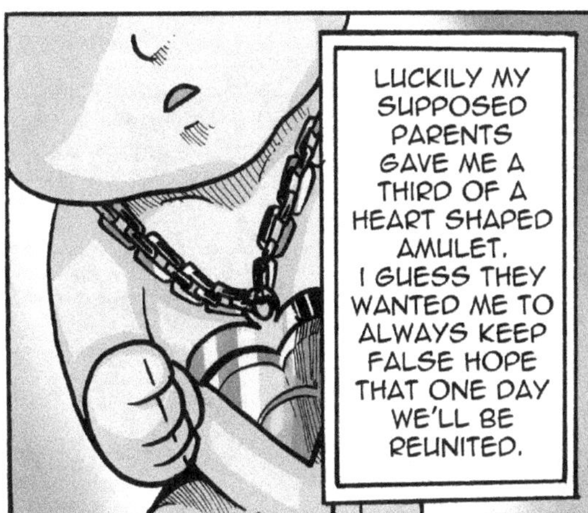
LUCKILY MY SUPPOSED PARENTS GAVE ME A THIRD OF A HEART SHAPED AMULET. I GUESS THEY WANTED ME TO ALWAYS KEEP FALSE HOPE THAT ONE DAY WE'LL BE REUNITED.

THROW
I WAS SHOT OUT THE WINDOW BY HER AT CONCEPTION. BAM! INSTANT ORPHAN!

MY CIRCUMS-TANTIAL BIRTH IS THE BEGINNING OF MY STORY, UNLESS YOU COUNT PAST LIVES OF COURSE.
IN WHICH CASE I WAS ABSOLUTELY A STRAY WOLF SEARCHING FOR PARADISE!

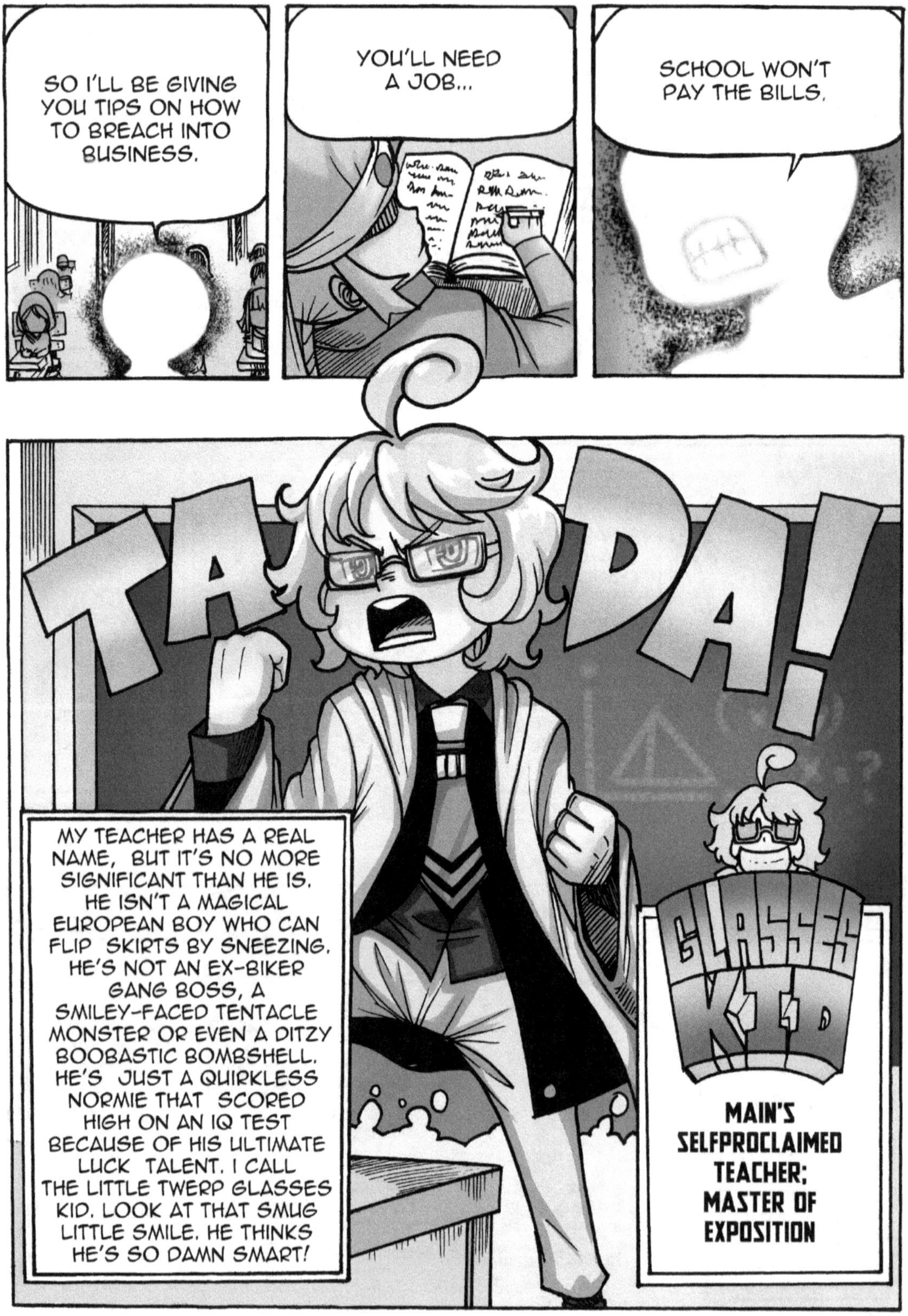

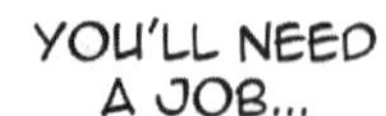

TA-DA!

MY TEACHER HAS A REAL NAME, BUT IT'S NO MORE SIGNIFICANT THAN HE IS. HE ISN'T A MAGICAL EUROPEAN BOY WHO CAN FLIP SKIRTS BY SNEEZING. HE'S NOT AN EX-BIKER GANG BOSS, A SMILEY-FACED TENTACLE MONSTER OR EVEN A DITZY BOOBASTIC BOMBSHELL. HE'S JUST A QUIRKLESS NORMIE THAT SCORED HIGH ON AN IQ TEST BECAUSE OF HIS ULTIMATE LUCK TALENT. I CALL THE LITTLE TWERP GLASSES KID. LOOK AT THAT SMUG LITTLE SMILE. HE THINKS HE'S SO DAMN SMART!

GLASSES KID

MAIN'S SELFPROCLAIMED TEACHER; MASTER OF EXPOSITION

EH, BUT ENOUGH ABOUT THE SHORT STACK. LET'S TALK MORE ABOUT BEST FRIEND – THE ONLY ONE BESIDES ME WHO ACTUALLY MATTERS! HE'S A LITTLE BIT...TOTALLY SUICIDAL. IN FACT, HE TOLD ME NUMEROUS TIMES THAT HE LIVES ON ONLY BECAUSE OF HIS TRAGIC PAST. UNTIL HE FULFILLS SOME VAGUE GOAL, HE WON'T BE ABLE TO DIE IN PEACE. I HAVE A FEELING HIS GOAL IS TO FINALLY GRADUATE FROM THE THIRD GRADE.

MAN, I REALLY AM A GREAT FRIEND. BUT I CAN'T TAKE IT ANYMORE! I HAVE TO ESCAPE THIS ***IMPEL DAWN.*** I'VE TRIED TO BURN DOWN THE SCHOOL SEVERAL TIMES, BUT I ALWAYS GET CAUGHT.

THAT'S WHY I'VE STOLEN HIS TEXTBOOKS AND SET FIRE TO HIS SCANTRONS.

WE'RE GOING TO DO IT! AND THEN WE'RE GOING TO GET MARRIED AND HAVE A TON OF KIDS!

THAT'S WHY I DECIDED TO FINALLY STUDY. THIS IS GOING TO BE THE YEAR I GRADUATE AND FULFILL MY DREAM OF GOING TO TOKYO U! BF AND I MADE A PROMISE TO PASS TOGETHER.

AND NOW LET ME INTRODUCE YOU TO THE FINAL IMPORTANT CHARACTER.

BOOBS

SUCCUBUS QUEEN TURNED LOVE PILLOW BY CURSED WATERMELON; MAIN'S ETERNAL WAIFU FOREVA AND EVA AND EVA

BEING THE MASTER WORDSMITH THAT I AM, I'VE DECIDED TO CALL HER BOOBS. SHE'S EIGHTEEN BECAUSE I SAY SO AND SHE'S A NATURAL BLONDE. SHE ALWAYS WHISPERS SWEET NOTHINGS TO ME WHENEVER I NEED HER. AND BY THAT, I MEAN SHE DOESN'T SAY ANYTHING. SHE IS A PILLOW, AFTER ALL.

SURE, SHE'S GRAFTED ONTO A STICKY HUG PILLOW, BUT THAT DOESN'T CHANGE THAT WE'VE WATCHED FIRE-WORKS, SUNSETS, SNUGGLE EVERY NIGHT AND BEST OF ALL SHE NEVER TELLS ME ABOUT HER FEELINGS. I DON'T ACTUALLY KNOW WHAT ANIME SHE'S FROM, PROBABLY SOMETHING REALLY NICHE BUT AWESOME LIKE ***ASSAULT ON TITAN.***

ONE DAY I WILL HAVE TO ABANDON HER SADLY. I MUST GROW MORE POWERFUL IF I AM TO DEFEAT THE NHK.

GLARE...
OTAKU

HAHAHAHAHA
BREASTS AND WOMEN SHOULD HAVE NO POWER OVER MAIN CHARACTER!

I BELIEVE IN YOU, MAIN. I KNOW YOU STUDIED HARD.
OH CRAP! GLASSES KID IS CALLING OUT OUR GRADES! I BETTER PAY ATTENTION.

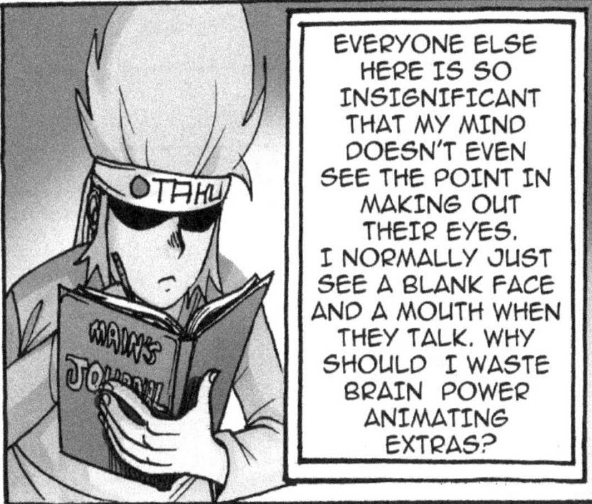
OTAKU
EVERYONE ELSE HERE IS SO INSIGNIFICANT THAT MY MIND DOESN'T EVEN SEE THE POINT IN MAKING OUT THEIR EYES. I NORMALLY JUST SEE A BLANK FACE AND A MOUTH WHEN THEY TALK. WHY SHOULD I WASTE BRAIN POWER ANIMATING EXTRAS?

WAIT, SHE BELIEVES IN ME... I NEED TO INTRODUCE HER. I'M ANIMATING HER EYES IN. OKAY. SHE HAS HAIR COVERING HER EYE AND ITS COLOR IS...

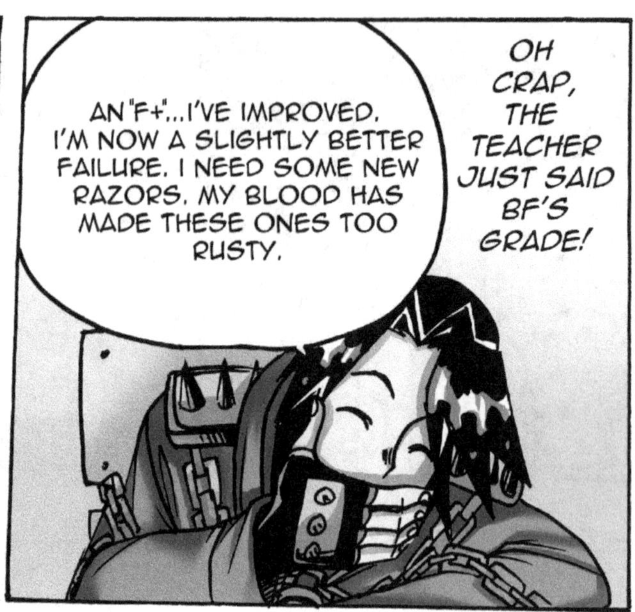

WHAT IF I PASS? I DON'T WANT TO GRADUATE WITHOUT HIM! WHO WILL GIVE ME KISSES GOODNIGHT? WHO WILL WASH MY BACK WITH HIS TOUNGE? AND WHO WILL MASSAGE MY EGO!? DAMN IT, I WON'T EVEN HAVE A WARM BODY TO CUDDLE NAKED WITH WHEN THE ORPHANAGE GETS COLD.

ALRIGHT, AFTER ALL...THERE'S STILL SOMETHING I MUST ACCOMPLISH.
LET'S PROMISE TO GRADUATE TOGETHER...
AND ACTUALLY DO IT THIS TIME!

TOSS
BLAG

WE STOOD THERE LOCKED IN EACH OTHER'S ENTRACING GAZE LIKE THE QUEER HETERO ICE SKATERS FROM *YAOI ON ICE*.

UM... WHO ARE YOU AGAIN, GIRLIE?
SHE MAY BE TAKING UP MY SCREEN TIME, BUT SHE IS TALKING ABOUT ME. I GUESS I SHOULD GIVE HER A NAME. SOMETHING ABOUT HER FEELS KINDA FAMILIAR.

DON'T WORRY, I KNOW YOU CAN DO IT! I'VE WATCHED YOU STUDY AND I KNOW YOU'LL MAKE IT.

SO, STALKER, WHAT WAS THE PROMISE?
OTAKU

WHO THE HELL IS THIS GIRL? SHE SAYS SHE'S MY CHILDHOOD FRIEND. GOOD THING I ALWAYS HAVE A GUN WITH ME INSIDE BOOBS.
I'M YOUR CHILDHOOD FRIEND.
I WON'T EVER FORGET THE PROMISE YOU MADE THAT DAY.
I'VE DONE EVERYTHING SO I CAN BECOME SOMEONE WORTHY OF YOUR FEELINGS.

WAIT HER SEAT WAS RIGHT IN FRONT OF ME?! AND IT'S FACING ME! HOW LONG HAS SHE BEEN HERE? EITHER WAY, IT LOOKS LIKE SHE'S GOING TO GRADUATE. LUCKILY LITTLE BRAT GOT AN "A+".

YOU DO REMEMBER!

I GUESS I SHOULD ADD HER TO THE CHARACTER ROSTER. I DON'T MIND HAVING ANOTHER ADORING FAN, ESPECIALLY ONE WHO ACTS LIKE A TYPICAL GIRL FROM A ROMANCE ANIME. YEAH, I KNOW I'M FAR BEYOND COMMON TROPES, BUT THE FACT THAT SHE'S ACTING THIS WAY IN REAL LIFE MAKES HER UNIQUE IN MY EYES.
TADA
STALKER
CLASS PRESIDENT OF THE MAIN CHARACTER FANCLUB; POSSIBLY MY CHILDHOOD FRIEND

YEP. EVERY DAY SINCE THE FIRST GRADE.
NO. THAT'S NOT CREEPY AT ALL.
NODS

WAIT, WE'VE DONE THAT BEFORE?
SO, DO YOU WANT TO WALK HOME TOGETHER AGAIN?

SHE LIVES WITH ME? THIS IS INSANE! JUST WHO THE HELL IS THIS GIRL? GEEZ, SHE'S LIKE YUNO GORESAI! BUT THE NON-LEGAL VERSION. WHICH DELETES THE ONLY REASON TO MAKE HER MY GIRLFRIEND!

WHERE DO YOU LIVE?
WHY WITH YOU OF COURSE, DARLING.

WHEN DID WE MEET?
YOU'RE A LEGEND! THE MAIN CHARACTER!
I'VE WATCHED ALL YOUR VIDEOS AND I'M ALWAYS THE FIRST TO COMMENT.

ARE YOU
ANGELLOLIPOP8?
THANK GOODNESS, SHE'S JUST A FANGIRL. I CAN HANDLE THIS.

THANKS FOR ALL THE SUPPORT.
YOU'RE WELCOME. THIS IS SO AWESOME! AWESOME! AWESOME!!!
YUPPERS!
AWW, SHE'S NOT SO BAD. SHE'S MY NUMBER ONE PATRON. SHE'S BEEN A FAN SINCE OUR VERY FIRST VIDEO. IT'S ACTUALLY REALLY COOL MEETING HER IN PERSON. TOO BAD SHE ISN'T A TOTAL HOTTIE WITH A SEXY BURN MARK.

WHAT WAS YOUR FAVORITE VIDEO REVIEW?
KODOMO NO CHIKAN!

....
?

WHAT IS CUTE IN ANIME IS REALLY CREEPY IN REAL LIFE.
WHISPER
WHISPER
WHISPER
HEY MASTER, GUESS WHAT ...

DEEP BREATHS MAIN, FOCUS YOUR **NEN**. SHE'S JUST A KID...
UGH, BUT THAT'S THE PROBLEM!
ALRIGHT, JUST A FEW MINUTES LEFT AND THEN ITS BEACH TIME. BEST FRIEND AND I WILL SPLASH EACH OTHER WITH WATER WHILE GIGGLING LIKE LITTLE GIRLS.
THEN WE'LL RUB OIL ON EACH OTHER'S BACKS WITH OUR BARE BODIES. AFTER THAT WE'LL CHASE ALL THE CHICKS IN SWIMSUITS!
AND WHEN THAT'S OVER WE'LL SPEND THE NIGHT IN A HOTEL. WE'LL BE PILLOW FIGHTING TILL THE SUN COMES UP!

KRAKOOM!!
WELL, WELL, LOOK AT THE TIME. THE BELL SHOULD RING ANY MOMENT AND THEN IT'S UMI TIME! I JUST HOPE THE OMINOUS SWIRLING STORMY CLOUDS OUTSIDE AREN'T A PREMONITION OF WHAT'S TO COME. OH WELL, THERE'S ONLY A MINUTE LEFT OF CLASS. WHAT COULD POSSIBLY HAPPEN?
TO BE CONTINUED...

CONCEPT ART

MEET THE TEAM

SPHERE OF COMPASSION

Sphere of Compassion was created in 2015. The goals of the company are to reinvigorate storytelling, inspire innovation, combat anthropocentrism and inspire others to be more openminded and live more compassionately towards people of all species.

Alexander McCarty is the writer and president of Sphere of Compassion Inc. He first began writing the *Of The Exps* series in 7th grade and has been working on it ever since. As a longtime fan of anime, manga, video games, Indi books and comics, he pools together ideas that he likes and then gives them a twist to create unique characters, storylines and abilities. Alex is a proud Vegan animal liberation activist and hopes to open the minds of his readers with his diverse cast of psychologically rich characters. He is a lifetime learner and loves making his friends and family laugh. Having graduated from college with a focus on Asian and Religious Studies, he now keeps up a daily regimen of meeting his own writing quotas. He listens to any and all comments, suggestions, reflections and criticism.

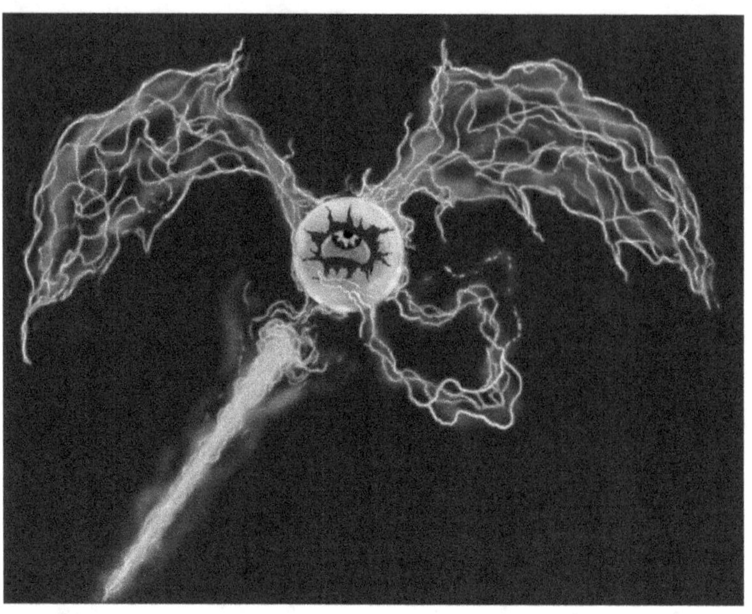

Gabriel McCarty is the vice president of Sphere of Compassion. Their roles in the company include head artist, concept designer, character designer and editor. Together with their brother, they co-created *Of The Exps & The Main Character* series. As a lover of nature and all living things, they are a Vegan animal liberation activist who is always looking to improve their methods of activism and education. They graduated from FIU with a BFA in Game Design and strives to educate and inspire others through their creations. They are a longtime fan of anime, manga, videogames and comics and is inspired by many of the great artist in these fields to create the most interesting, unique and deep characters. They strive for originality and intrigue in their works and is always looking to learn something new, have fun and meet new people.

KAPUMAX INTERVIEW

ALEX & GABRIEL: Welcome to ***Sphere Of Compassion Interviews!*** Today we will be introducing you to the artist behind the ***The Main Character! The Manga!*** We are talking about the mangaka ***Kapumax!***

GABRIEL: Kapumax is currently working on 3 ongoing projects: ***The Main Character! The Manga!***; the already published manga ***Fallen Angel*** (written by Deandre); and his own manga ***Berserking!***

ALEX: Kapumax's patience and hard work is really on a completely different level! Based on the information we've received, he loved to draw ever since he was a child. In 2018 he began accepting works from foreign countries! It's so exciting to learn more about Kapumax!

GABRIEL: It's better if we welcome our artist to know more about him and his journey of being a manga artist! **PLEASE WELCOME KAPUMAX!!!**

KAPUMAX: Good day Sir Alex and Gabriel, and of course to our dear readers.

ALEX: A Good Day to you also, Kapumax. It's our pleasure to have you as our guest, especially considering you have a hectic schedule.

KAPUMAX: The pleasure is all mine, the truth is, I advanced the sketches of our next chapter a week before this show that's why I'm sure I won't be late for our deadline.

GABRIEL: Wow, you are really prepared for this day!

KAPUMAX: Maybe a little bit, Hahaha!

ALEX: Hahaha! So now let's start the interview! I am so excited to learn more about you! We're going to ask some questions from our readers!

KAPUMAX: My health statistics aren't included, are they? Hahaha

GABRIEL: Haha! Don't worry, all of the questions are concerning you as a mangaka!

KAPUMAX: Sounds great!

ALEX: Question one: Out of all the professions and jobs out there, some with much higher salary, why choose to be a mangaka Is this your dream job?

KAPUMAX: I started drawing in kindergarten. While growing up my admiration for art grew also. Even though I am currently an employee working in the daytime, I still make plenty of time to work on my passion as a manga artist!

GABRIEL: You work so hard! I can't imagine having to keep up with three mangas while juggling a daytime job too! We salute you!

ALEX: Absolutely! Now, for the second question. You've seen hundreds of manga and anime like we have! What manga or anime inspired you to make manga? Who are the creators that inspired you!

KAPUMAX: In High School, many anime series caught my attention and I idolized dozens of creators! I had difficulty finding my art-style because I kept adapting their art-style when I drew. Eventually, I filtered through them one by one and chose the best one for me. The manga/anime ***One Piece*** is my greatest inspiration. Many people say I have the same art style as ***Eichiro Oda*** but I am gradually changing it more and more into my own original art style.

GABRIEL: You're already there, my friend! Now for the second to last question. What tips would you give to an aspiring manga artist in this era?

KAPUMAX: The greatest lesson I can pass on is the importance of the "speed of implementation". If you want to be a great artist someday, you absolutely must start now and keep at it every day! You must also increase the pace at which you complete drawings! Challenge yourself and always be open to try new things! You will always grow! Life is too short and mastering your craft takes many years.

ALEX: Excellent answer! I know many aspiring artists can learn from your wise words. Final question: how do you envision your life as a manga artist will be ten years from now?

KAPUMAX: I envision it as my fulltime career! I will be a much better artist in ten years and will have ten or more volumes of my own manga! I am already at a different stage of my life, considering I am working with writers outside of my home in the Philippines. I hope to have helped other manga artists like the ones who helped me by the end of the decade.

GABRIEL: We know that you will absolutely accomplish your dreams! Thank you, Kapumax! We've learned so much from you and will continue to be inspired by you! We are truly blessed to have you working on our project alongside us!

KAPUMAX: It's an absolute pleasure working on ***The Main Character! The Manga!*** project. I am very happy to be able to bring new life to your work!

ALEX: Our dear readers, this is unfortunately the end of this program.

GABRIEL: Thanks for reading and we hope you've enjoyed and learned in this edition of...

ALEX & GABRIEL: ***Sphere of Compassion Interviews!***

AISA HA INTERVIEW

"I am a digital artist. I love drawing fan-art more than anything because I get to reimagine the characters in different forms and scenarios! I love reading manga and watching anime. I am an I.T graduate and I'm currently assisting with "TMC" manga as the colorist. My art style is free form, though I am more influenced by some fan artist as well like Hews, ID-Hyury, Wyen and many more. I also do animation as a hobby like animated GIFs." – Aisa Ha

Why did you choose to be a writer/artist?
I never thought I'd become an artist. It all started in grade school when Pokémon was still my favorite show. I'd tune in every day at 7:30 PM on cartoon network, and I just love the designs of every Pokémon! One day I decided to draw Pikachu, then some legendary Pokémon! I noticed that I was still drawing Pokémon until high school, and I've tried different styles since then. Now I'm still exploring a lot of things. I guess what pushes me to be an artist is the feeling of accomplishment when you see how your art turns out after it's all done.

When did you start writing stories and creating art?
It started when I was still in grade school; I usually draw Pokémon, Dragon Ball, Naruto and many other classic anime.

Who are your main inspirations?
I'm not really inspired by someone. I'm inspired by the arts that I see on the internet and how they find various ways to create different feelings for their artworks.

What are your favorite anime/manga?
My favorite anime is Code Geass and Attack on Titan. When I was little, I used to really like Pokémon, I still like it but not like when I was little. I also like Full Metal Alchemist Brotherhood, Shaman King and many more.

What are your typical styles in art creation?
I'm still in the process of finding my own signature art style. I sometimes draw portraits but I'm more of an anime-style artist.

How do you create your works?
I think of a scenario first and the mood. After that I draw a lot of sketches and decide to focus on that one sketch that I'm most connected with.

Sphere of Compassion Interview

Why did you choose to be a writer/artist?
Alex: I had so much free time in middle school and I felt I was just wasting it. So, I decided to start writing a book series and finished the first before the end of the school year. Pokémon the First movie was what originally inspired me since I was always bothered by the whole exploitation of Pokémon and how Mewtwo failed to go against that exploitation. I started writing with the intent to bring new worldviews to light.

Gabriel: I always loved to draw and create as a child and seeing all the cool characters and stories on TV and literature inspired me to create original worlds and characters. I enjoyed nothing more than creating my own dragons, aliens, technologies etc. and was always coming up with crazy expansive stories in my head, on paper or with my toys.

When did you start writing stories and creating art?
Alex: It's been over fifteen years since I began writing *Of the Exps*. I wrote in composition notebooks which improved my handwriting exponentially. *The Main Character* series began seven years ago, starting with a parody anime song.

Gabriel: Ever since I was able to hold a marker or crayon, I was drawing dinosaurs, dragons, and alien creatures on whatever I could get away with drawing on. I've gone to numerous art schools in my life from a preschool to collage and have always loved creating characters and worlds.

Who are your main inspirations?
Alex: I'm more so inspired by stories than individuals, but if there is one writer in particular who inspired me early on. Lemony Snicket (creator of *A Series of Unfortunate Events*) always had such a unique style of narration and always kept things fun. He also had thirteen books in his series, which made me aspire to write a massive epoch. Kazuki Takahashi (creator of *Yu-Gi-Oh!*) is another big early influencer for me. Manga artists in general really inspire me with their dedication and love for their art. Video games inspire me too of course! The Legacy of Kain, BlazBlue, Xenosaga, Final Fantasy, and Disgaea are among my top influences.

Gabriel: As far as humans go, I have many inspirations but I have a few core inspirations in my life. As far as storytelling goes Michael Crichton was an inspiration to me since I saw the first Jurassic Park movie. As a dinosaur nut, almost since birth, I read the novels shortly after the movie and then went on to his other works. The way he created realistic yet to be created technologies and blended horror with adventure in such a fun way inspired me to do the same. As far as visual art goes the horrifyingly beautiful and techno-Organic creations of H.R. Giger particularly his creation of the Xenomorphs from the Aliens series inspired my obsession with intricate details and technology in my art (I had a fun childhood). Other than that, the godfather of all things anime and manga Osamu Tezuka and many other mangakas have been my main inspiration as a young adult such as Satoshi Urushihara, Shirow Masamune and Kentaro Miura.

What are your favorite anime/manga?
Alex: My favorite anime fluctuates, but it's probably JoJo's Bizarre Adventure. I really love the unique abilities and just how stylish the show is. As for manga, Terra Formars! Excellent in characters, story-telling, action, science, art, and intrigue. Battle Royale is another favorite of mine and I still want a proper anime adaption for it to this day! My favorite movie is Watchmen and I love the graphic novel too of course. As for non anime shows, Shera and the Princesses of Power is both beloved by me and has been very influential, especially for *The Main Character* series.
Gabriel: My favorite anime's are Queens Blade, Hokuto no Ken, Blassrieter, and Fairy Tail. My favorite mangas are Konjiko no Gash Bell, Elfen Lied,

Gantz, Needless, Mahou Sensei Negima, and Seikon no Qwaser, Queensblade's godly music, legendary character development, and gorgeous art, some done by the king of sparkles Satoshi Urushihara himself, make it my favorite ecchi of all time. JoJo's Bizarre Adventure, Terra Formars, pre-timeskip One Piece and Yu Yu Hakusho are both great anime and manga with Terra Formars being the best manga I have ever read and my #1 favorite for its amazing action, storytelling, use of science, politics, art and well just about everything! Videogame series BlazeBlue, Legacy of Kain and Makai Senki Disgaea are some of my largest inspirations for style, storytelling and character design.

What are your typical styles in story writing and art creation?
Alex: I love to mix things up and challenge myself with complicated characters, new genres and just challenging scenarios in general. That said my main style is psychological dark fantasy. I love writing dialogue and action scenes the most. If I don't know what a character should say, I can often just act them out to figure out the proper movement or dialogue. Writing is truly a transformative journey. It's a really wonderful feeling when my own story outcome surprises me.

Gabriel: I like to think of who the character is and then design them as fun and crazy looking as I can. I usually have a very techno organic look and feel to my characters and designs. I love highly detailed armors, creatures, suits and weapons and love combining technology with humanistic, other worldly or demonic entities. I love to draw energies and effects like auras, fire, and liquids emanating from my creations. I love sharp pointed lines and designs like claws and horns and usually have many of them in my designs. I love interconnecting almost mazelike deigns in armors, structures and effects. I also have an obsession with multiple eyes or eyelike shapes such as orbs. Combining fantasy elements with science and the otherworldly features is my obsession!

How do you do your works?

Alex: I always plan out the entire book before I begin. Every part and chapter is set up ahead of time, but I'm also open to changing things should the need occur. *Guardian Angel* was planned to end at a much later point in the timeline, but that got moved to *Broad-Spectrum Assassin*. Every day (approximately) I sit down and write till I either finished a new chapter or finished planning out the next section in more detail. I keep tons of notes and I definitely add things as I go along. I'm not one for cutting out dialogue or scenes which is something I must learn to master for the sake of future manga releases.

Gabriel: As the head designer of our company, I try to find a base design and theme that best represents our series and company and keep trying till I feel it resonates with me. I look to the works from some of my favorite artists and companies to try to pick out layout designs and themes from the best of them and combine them with our own themes to create the most consistent awesome designs. In character design I often think of the character themselves first, whether from my own imagination or my brother's and try to discern what look goes with their personality, abilities and philosophies. I then look for references online or around me to best design the details that I'm looking for. I have a bit of a bad habit of making overly complicated and heavy detail designed characters but I always make sure the look fits them and keep trying until I'm happy with them and know that this is who they are. Other times I just start randomly drawing things and then realize its works perfectly for a character.

Books from ***Sphere of Compassion***

THE MAIN CHARACTER!

Hero's Epic Journey Arc

A Subversive PUNCH to the Face!

Join Main Character and Best Friend, two proud American otakus and ViralTube legends, who are pulled into another world and bribed into joining a growing conflict between victimized villages and deranged dictators. Anime tropes only lead to shattered expectations for our ego-driven hero! He is accompanied by awesome allies, protected by canonical plot armor, and armed with the power of Friendship (a vulgar rocket launcher who uses emotions as ammo). But will these and his encyclopedic knowledge of anime be enough to overcome the threats of a dimension hopping assassin, a guardian angel's sexual advances, a musclebound amazonian, memory erasing mushrooms, a Fearsome Dragon, a charismatic king with a psychotic obsession for our hero and his army of cut throat cat boys?

The Main Character is a 4th wall breaking parody packed with anime references, subversive characters and intense battles!

Be your own Hero!

Before she found the Hero of Destiny, Annie had her own journey!

Join Annie on her adventure through the epic dark fantasy world of The Main Character series! This young, loving and determined girl will team up with cursed heroes, adorable angels and mythical creatures to re-unite with her cherished family! Will her bonds with her allies be enough to protect her from mechanized samurai, shadow hounds, rogue dimensional assassins and an army of CatBoy soldiers? Or will life's story be closed before she can write her happily ever after?

This book can be read before OR after any book from ***The Main Character*** *series.*

A SUPLEX of Subversion!

Main Character and Best Friend, two legendary otaku heroes, are back in action.

They now have a diverse group of otherworldly allies: a guardian angel Stalker, a shy Brawny Babe, a Tomboy CatGirl, a Fruity-scented fortune teller, a foul-mouthed bazooka of Friendship and a freaking Harem of strong female leads! Juggling his harem is the least of his worries though. This time he'll have to go head to head against a psychotic Rival, a mind-manipulating Mascot, a mysterious organization, a blackmailing midget, and horny Harem girls? Even with Point of View manipulation, the ability to Retcon his failures and hair that can punch your lights out, can Main Character overcome his own ego and become a true hero? Or will his backlog of bad choices create a rift between him and his allies?

The Main Character is still a 4th wall breaking parody packed with anime references, subversive characters and intense battles! This time around it also has a Harem of lovely ladies to give it new vigor!

In a School of Assassins, Suffering is Growth.

Before Assailant encountered the Hero of Destiny, he crafted his own legend!

Discover the dark origins of the fabled Broad-Spectrum assassin. Follow him through deadly exams, covert conspiracies and murderous missions all the while delving deep into the lore of the epic dark fantasy world of The Main Character series! This child of misfortune will work alongside cuddly killers, polymorphous monsters, enslaved heroes, and tragic angels to unravel the secrets hidden by the Assassin's Guild. Armed with mythic knowledge and guided by love, can he wield his truth to conquer skillful students, treacherous assassins, shadowy shapeshifters and secret organizations? Will his legends become a beacon of hope or a seed of despair?

This book can be read before OR after any book from ***The Main Character*** *series.*

OF THE EXPS

Rebellion Arc

Freedom is a Shackle.

Exp 8 is a living weapon. After awakening in an isolated lab, one instinct fuels him: a burning desire for freedom. His creator, Devlin, will stop at nothing to keep Exp 8 subservient to his will, even if it means sending droves of weaponized warriors to capture him. To break out of Devlin's hold, Exp 8 stages a rebellion, using both his wit and power to unite his fellow Exps against their creator. But not all enemies can be converted, and Devlin is not the only one with plans for the rogue weapon. The sentient inventions Exp 8 and his allies encounter become more powerful, fanatical and merciless with each wave. Driven by instinct and the desire to free his people, Exp 8 perseveres through conflict and loss. Is freedom worth the cost if he alone desires it?

A sci-fi anime-style experience packed with intense battles and other-worldly abilities.

Resurrection Arc

True Heroes are Created, not Born.

This is the story of Exp 8, an artificial life-form who died in the pursuit of freedom. Exp 8 awakes in the afterlife and sets out on a mission to dethrone the tyrant king of Sel and free the tortured residents from systemic slavery. Unable to defeat the god alone, he must unite a demonic rebel army, locate his fallen comrades, and convince gods to join his cause. Even with old enemies and new allies at his side, can he overcome the God of Hate and become the Hero of Sel?

An action fantasy anime-style experience that explores the afterlife and the gods who shape it.

Origins of the Exps

Is clairvoyance a gift or a curse?

Before she became Fate, Ebui fought against her destiny.

Explore the ancient culture and traditions of the Ainu through the lens of a child. Ebui is a hopeful and brave girl who yearns to become a respected shaman of her village. Threats loom around every chapter of her life in the form of enemy tribes, violent ceremonies, sinister plots, and her own cursed prophecies. Will her hope survive through the supernatural storm of despair, or will her efforts bring about the end of her people?

Immerse yourself in the lives and backstories of characters from the *Of The Exps* series in the first of the Origins of the Exps novels!

This book can be read before any book from ***Of The Exps*** *series.*

FUTURE RELEASES

Rise Arc

***Eternal Rival*: Rise of the Exps** (Summer 2020)

Does competition encourage growth or ensue destruction?

After the aftermath of the realm god death matches, new gods are selected. Kaity's new responsibilities clash with her desire to save her friends, further dividing her already splintered forces. Despite already being overwhelmed by Sel's Pawns and the Exp Hunters, new factions emerge that are hellbent on claiming the power of Sellum for themselves. The young God of the Afterlife must forge new alliances to survive. Can she placate her enemies by reaching a common ground? Or is their thirst for power beyond negotiation?

The third arc of the action-packed sci-fi anime-style novel series will bring the divine conflict to Earth!

Escapades of the Exps

Intimate Interrogation (Fall 2020)

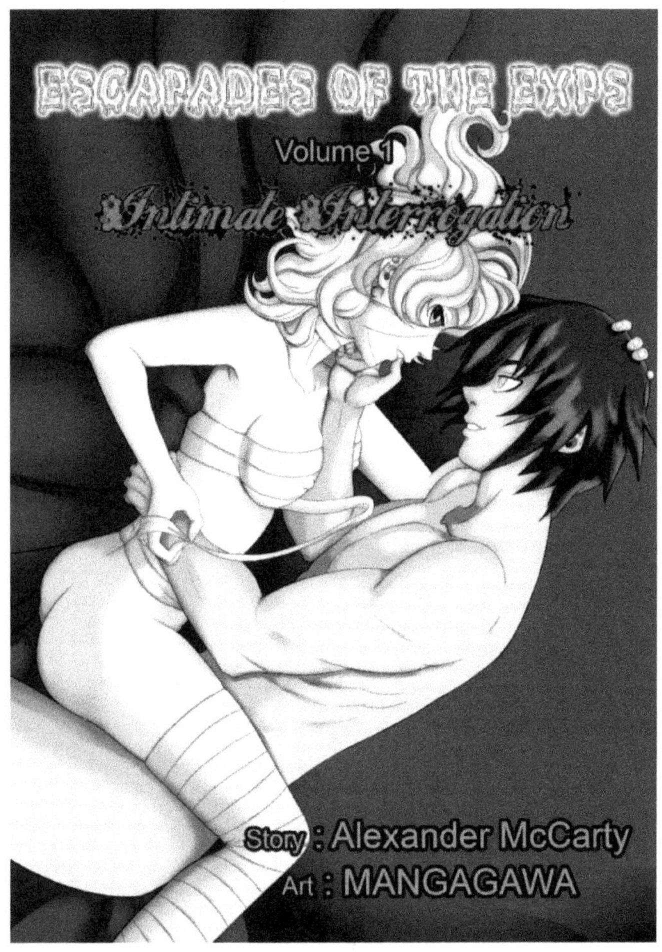

Is sex just another tool for an assassin?

The deadly girlfriend of Devlin's new crush is discovered in his bed. The seductive assassin has an offer for the hot-blooded scientist and will do whatever she must to seduce him to her cause.

Become entranced by the first Hentai Manga from ***Of The Exps*** series based on a scene from the ***Rebellion of the Exps: Exp 8*** novel.

*This manga can be read before any book from **Of The Exps** series.*

READ THE FULL COLOR NOW BY SIGNING UP ON

https://Patreon.com/Sphere_of_Compassion/

Best Friend's Special Message

In this world, there are the victims and the victimizers. If you believe it's wrong to harm the innocent, then don't do it. Animals of all species have cherished families. Freedom is their birthright. I don't want Main's fans to cheer on his heroic acts while hypocritically contributing to needless animal exploitation and death. Be your own hero and live with integrity. Live Vegan and inspire others to do the same!

Living a vegan life is the moral way to treat our fellow animals with the respect they deserve. We need to take responsibility and stand against the exploitation and enslavement of our fellow living beings by transitioning to a VEGAN lifestyle. We can all make a difference in the lives of those who are enslaved and executed for not being born human. Every time we make a purchase, we are casting a vote which either supports or opposes exploitation and violence. If we follow our ethics by living vegan, we can end systemic slavery worldwide!

If you seek resources, the ones below are the absolute best.

http://www.adaptt.org/

http://www.abolitionistapproach.com/

veganeducationgroup.com

www.ingramcontent.com/pod-product-compliance
Lightning Source LLC
LaVergne TN
LVHW080316110826
845155LV00023B/132

* 9 7 8 1 9 4 3 7 3 3 2 3 1 *